ALIS[...] DARE

LITTLE MISS ADVENTURES

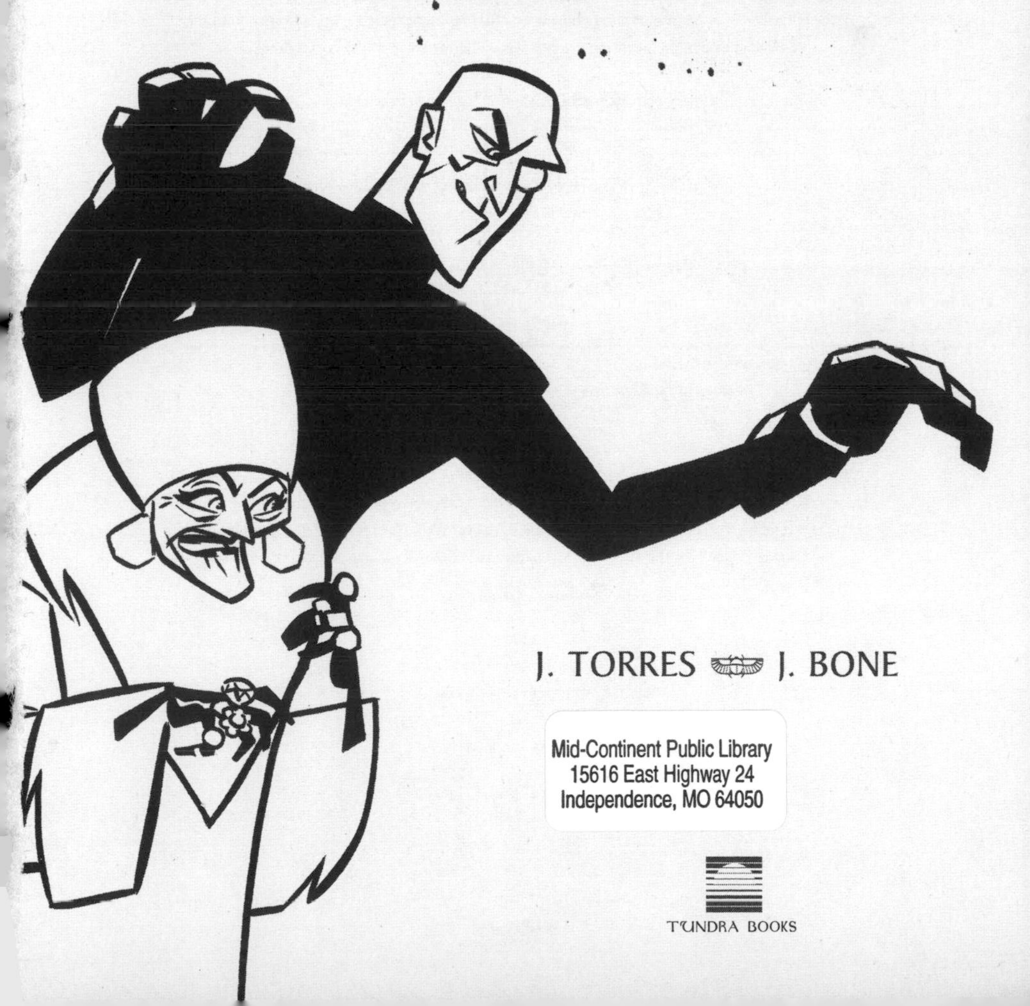

J. TORRES J. BONE

TUNDRA BOOKS

Published in Canada by Tundra Books,
75 Sherbourne Street, Toronto, Ontario M5A 2P9

Published in the United States by Tundra Books of Northern New York,
P.O. Box 1030, Plattsburgh, New York 12901

Library of Congress Control Number: 2009929063

Library and Archives Canada Cataloguing in Publication

Torres, J., 1969-
Alison Dare, little Miss Adventures / J. Torres ; J.
Bone, illustrator.

Previously published as v. 1. of Alison Dare, little Miss Adventures.
ISBN 978-0-88776-934-4

I. Bone, J. (Jason) II. Title.

PS8639.O78A65 2010 j741.5'971 C2009-905064-1

We acknowledge the financial support of the Government of Canada through the Book Publishing Industry Development Program (BPIDP) and that of the Government of Ontario through the Ontario Media Development Corporation's Ontario Book Initiative. We further acknowledge the support of the Canada Council for the Arts and the Ontario Arts Council for our publishing program.

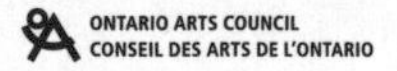

Design by Jennifer Lum

Cover illustration by J. Bone

Printed and bound in Canada

1 2 3 4 5 6 15 14 13 12 11 10

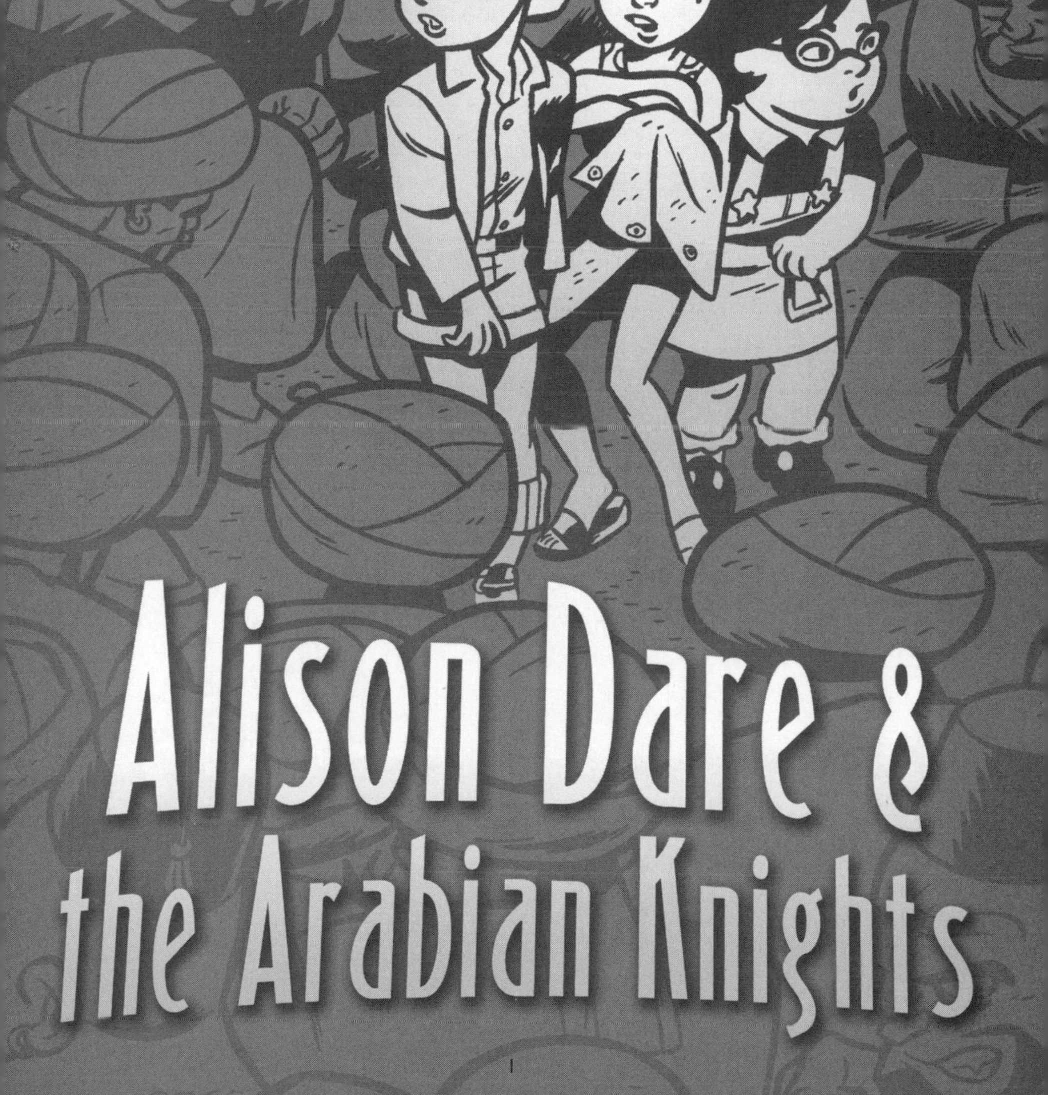
Alison Dare &
the Arabian Knights

Arabia Felix
ONCE UPON A TIME...
Arabian Sea
IN THE EXPANSIVE SULTANATE OF SHAHRAZAD...
WITHIN THE ARID REGION OF ES-SINDIBAD...
JUST OUTSIDE THE ANCIENT CITY OF ALA-ED-DIN.

THERE WAS A BORED LITTLE GIRL NAMED
ALISON DARE

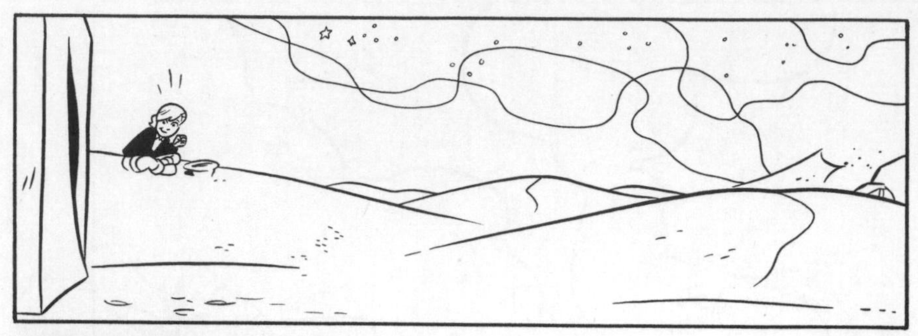

"FROM THE LAND BEYOND, BEYOND FROM THE WORLD PAST HOPE AND FEAR, I BID YOU, GENIE, NOW APPEAR."

ONE DAY, THE BORED GIRL MET AN EQUALLY BORED GENIE.
YAWN!
SCRITCH
SCRITCH
Poof
BOTH WERE QUITE EXCITED TO SEE THE OTHER.
BOTH WERE CONVINCED THEY HAD WAITED AGES FOR SOME EXCITEMENT.
BOTH WERE EAGER TO FIND AMUSEMENT WITH THE OTHER'S HELP...
I DON'T UNDERSTAND WHAT YOU'RE SAYING--
--BUT I KNOW THE DRILL.
MY FIRST WISH: BRING WENDY AND DOT HERE!
AND THUS BEGAN ALISON DARE'S ARABIAN NIGHTS (MIS)ADVENTURE...

SIM SIM SALA

BIM!
ALISON...?

WELCOME TO SHAHRAZAD, GIRLS!
I MUST BE DREAMING.
MAYBE I SLIPPED IN THE POOL AND BUMPED MY HEAD.

NOPE. YOU'RE NOT IN A DREAM OR A COMA. I ASKED MY "SLAVE" OVER THERE TO BRING YOU HERE!
HOW COOL IS THAT!?

NOT COOL, ALISON. MY SISTER WAS TEACHING ME HOW TO DIVE!
I WAS PRACTICING IN MY ROOM JUST A SECOND AGO...

WHAT'S THE MATTER WITH YOU TWO?
I HAD TO SNEAK AROUND IN THE MIDDLE OF THE NIGHT WHILE EVERYONE WAS ASLEEP TO COPY THE RIGHT MAGIC WORDS OUT OF MY MOM'S JOURNAL!

AND I HAD TO WAIT FOR EVERYONE TO BE AWAY BEFORE TRYING OUT THE LAMP. LATER I'LL SHOW YOU THE OTHER COOL THINGS I FOUND. BUT FOR NOW, FORGET DIVING AND... TRIANG... ULATING!
YOUR REAL SPRING BREAK FUN STARTS NOW!

A WHOLE NEW WORLD OF ADVENTURE IS WAITING FOR US OUT THERE!

OH, YEAH...
I'M DREAMING
ALL RIGHT...

SNAP OUT
OF IT, HUH!?
I'VE GOT TWO WISHES
LEFT. HELP ME
DECIDE WHAT TO
ASK FOR...

AND TELL ME GENIE-ESE IS
ONE OF THE KAJILLION
LANGUAGES
YOU CAN SPEAK.
LAMP BOY
OVER THERE DOESN'T
DO ENGLISH.
SORRY,
NO!

HEY, WHAT ABOUT
YOUR PARENTS?
MY PARENTS?
THEY DON'T SPEAK
GENIE-ESE.
NO, I MEAN,
MAYBE WISHING
THEM BACK
TOGETHER.

oh...
HEY,
ALISON!

HOW ABOUT
WISHING ME
SOME
CLOTHES?

MY BAG'S
OVER THERE.
BORROW WHATEVER
YOU WANT. I'M
NOT WASTING
A WISH!
UH-UH. WE'VE GOT
THREE DAYS BEFORE
IT'S BACK TO SCHOOL.
I WANNA MAKE
THE MOST OF WHAT'S
LEFT OF OUR
VACATION.

THERE'S SO MUCH TO DO OUT HERE! I HAVE TO SHOW YOU GUYS THE ...UH... WELL, THERE'S... AND THE...
HOW'S THE SHOPPING?
HOW DOES THIS SOUND: A BAZAAR WITH SNAKE CHARMERS AND PEOPLE WALKING BAREFOOT ON HOT COALS! AND A CRAZY OLD MAN LYING ON A BED OF NAILS!
UH... GREAT.
THAT SETTLES IT, GENIE. WE DON'T WANT TO GO BACK TO SCHOOL SO SOON.
FOR MY SECOND WISH, I'D LIKE MORE TIME HERE IN SHAHRAZAD!
COME ON, GENIE WE'RE LOOKING FOR--
Swashbuckling ADVENTURE! DEATH DEFYING DANGER! --A LITTLE INTRIGUE! Romance! ACTION!
A LONGER SPRING BREAK SOUNDS GOOD TO ME.
GET IT, GENIE? GIVE US A FEW MORE DAYS HERE. NO, ANOTHER WEEK!
HOW ABOUT ANOTHER MONTH!
WHO'S WE?
I GOT IT! LIKE IN THE STORIES... 1001 ARABIAN NIGHTS!
SIM SIM SALA

BIM!
ALL HAIL THE SULTANA ALI-SON!

WHAT'S THIS? I DIDN'T ASK FOR THIS!
NOW I HOPE I'M DREAMING.
A-ARE THESE FRIENDS OF YOUR M-MOM, ALISON? WHAT'S GOING ON?
ALISON... I THINK MAYBE YOUR GENIE THOUGHT YOU WANTED 1001 KNIGHTS...
"KNIGHTS" WITH A "K"...
THAT'S RIDICULOUS! I SAID "LIKE IN THE STORY"! ARE THERE EVEN KNIGHTS WITH A "K" IN THE BOOK?
WELL, THE ARABIAN NIGHTS ARE A COLLECTION OF PERSIAN, ARABIAN AND EAST INDIAN FOLK TALES GATHERED THROUGHOUT THE MIDDLE AGES. THERE IS NO ONE "BOOK", BUT SEVERAL RE-TELLINGS, INCLUDING WESTERN ONES THAT REFER TO THE SULTAN'S SWORDSMEN, THE ROYAL GUARD IF YOU WILL, AS "KNIGHTS". THE MOST POPULAR VERSIONS HAVE A FRAMING DEVICE INVOLVING THE DAUGHTER OF A VIZIER USING ENGAGING STORYTELLING TO
OKAY! OKAY! GOT IT!
NO ONE ASKED FOR A BOOK REPORT!
NUDGE

HELLO?
DO SOMETHING ABOUT ALL THESE MEN...
I'M TRYING TO CHANGE OVER HERE!

DO NOT ADDRESS THE SULTANA IN THAT TONE!
HASSAN STOP!
GRR
AAAHH!

NO, HASSAN!
YOU STOP!
DON'T YOU DARE LAY A HAND ON MY FRIEND!
WAS IT SOMETHING I SAID?

AS YOU WISH, MISTRESS.
1001 PARDONS, SULTANA.

MEANWHILE...
GILLIAN...

PLEASE ASK THOSE GUYS TO MOVE OUT OF THE WAY.

UH... WHICH ONES, DR. DARE?
ALL OF--

...THEM?

BACK INSIDE...
I'D LIKE TO TRY ON SOME LOCAL COUTURE. CAN YOU GET ME SOME OF THOSE SILKY HANDKERCHIEFS TO WEAR ABOUT MY HEAD ALL MYSTERIOUS-LIKE?
THE SULTANA MEANS VEILS AND HEADSCARVES. ONLY THE FINEST SILK FOR YOU, MISTRESS.
WHAT ABOUT SOME OF THOSE BAGGY FLOW-Y BOTTOMS AND SHORT BELLY DANCER TOPS MY DAD WOULD NEVER LET ME WEAR?
THE SULTANA MEANS SHALWAR PANTALOONS AND BEDLAH SUITS. ONLY THE MOST AUTHENTIC, MISTRESS.
AND WHAT ABOUT SOME OF THOSE SHOES WITH THE POINTY TOES THAT CURL UPWARDS?
THE SULTANA MEANS ...THE SHOES WITH THE POINTY TOES THAT CURL UPWARDS.
ONLY THE...POINTIEST, MISTRESS.

HUNGRY, WENDY? WANNA TRY SOME LOCAL CUISINE?
I'VE READ THAT THIS AREA IS KNOWN FOR ITS PISTACHIO NUTS, PEARS, AND PLUMS...
YOU AND YOUR FRIENDS WILL FEAST TODAY, SULTANA-ALI-SON.
AND AFTER WE EAT, I'D LIKE TO TAKE MY FRIENDS SIGHTSEEING IN ALA-ED-DIN ...OR MAYBE WE'LL SEARCH FOR "THE CAVE OF WONDERS" ... POSSIBLY VENTURE AS FAR AS UBAR.
UBAR? THE "ATLANTIS OF THE SANDS"!
SO, WE'LL NEED SOME CAMELS.
AND...DO YOU THINK WE COULD DO SOMETHING ABOUT THIS UGLY OL' TENT?

WHERE DID THESE MEN COME FROM?
WHAT DO THEY WANT?

WELL, LADIES, YOU CAN ASK THEM YOURSELVES...

'CAUSE HERE THEY COME!

RUMBLE RUMBLE RUMBLE
RUMBLE
HAS ANYBODY SEEN ALISON LATELY?
RUMBLE

WE LEFT HER AT THE TENT.
DID YOU REMEMBER TO SECURE THE CRATE WITH ALL THE YOU-KNOW-WHATS?
UM...
I HAD TO FIX THE JEEP, SO I ASKED JOCK.
HEH... I HAD TO GET US MORE WATER BEFORE COMING OUT HERE ...BUT I COVERED THE CRATE WITH A SHEET ...HEH.
OH, LOOK! THEY'RE COMING BACK...
RUMBLE
RUMBLE
RUMBLE
RUMBLE
UMBLE
RUMBLE
RUMBLE
RUMBLE
RUMBLE

ALI-BABA, EAT YOUR HEART OUT!

FOR YOUR APPROVAL, SULTANA.

ALI-BABA...?
I HOPE NONE OF THIS STUFF IS STOLEN.

SO...HOW LONG BEFORE THE NEW TENT IS READY?

MAY IT BE WORTHY OF HER EXCELLENCY, ALI·SON...

oooh...
ahh...

ahem.

SO MUCH FOR THE LANGUAGE BARRIER, HUH?

LATER...
THIS IS NICE.

BUT HOW ABOUT SOME ACTIVITY?
THESE GUYS ARE KNIGHTS! ADVENTURE IS THEIR MIDDLE NAME
I COULD LIE HERE ALL DAY, ACTUALLY...

WHAT'S YOUR NAME? "MA ISMUK?"
ARWAAH.
ENGLISH TO ARAB DICTIONARY

HEY, POINDEXTER, DO YOU ALWAYS HAVE TO HAVE YOUR NOSE BURIED IN A BOOK?
IF I CAN'T DO ACTUAL ASSIGNED HOMEWORK WHILE I'M HERE, I MIGHT AS WELL DO SOME "INDEPENDENT STUDY."

BESIDES, I FOUND OUT THE GENIE'S NAME IS "ARWAAH."
WENDY...LIFE MOVES PRETTY FAST. IF YOU DON'T STOP AND LOOK AROUND ONCE IN AWHILE, YOU MIGHT MISS IT.

AND SO...
THE SULTANA WANTS TO GO FOR A CAMEL RIDE!
THE CAMELS!
FETCH THE CAMELS!
FETCH THE CAMELS!

FETCHING THE CAMELS!
FETCHING THE CAMELS!
BUMP
HEY, WATCH WHERE YOU'RE FETCHING!

oof!
EXCUSE ME!
HEY! WHERE'S THE FIRE?

...NO PUSHING...
HEY! THAT'S MY SISTER YOU'RE SHOVING, MISTER!
WE'RE JUST TRYING TO GET TO ALISON!

DID YOU HEAR THAT?
THEY'RE AFTER THE SULTANA!

WE MUST PROTECT ALI-SON!
HASSAN STOP NOW!
SEIZE THEM!

"SULTANA"?
"ALI-SON"?
WHAT HAS SHE DONE THIS TIME?

1001 APOLOGIES, SULTANA.
THERE HAS BEEN A... DELAY WITH THE ROYAL CAMELS.

DELAY?
EVERYTHING YOU EVER WANTED TO KNOW ABOUT GENIES BUT WERE AFRAID TO ASK!

I HATE WAITING AROUND!
GASP! THE SULTANA IS DISPLEASED!

MORE FOOD, MISTRESS? EAT, EAT, YOU'RE LOOKING THIN...

OOH, CHECK OUT THIS NEW OUTFIT, SULTANA!

PILLOW FIGHT ANYONE?

HOW ABOUT SOME ENTERTAINMENT...
WHAT THE...?!
CLAP CLAP
SNAP!
TOING CLONG
THEY TRACKED DOWN CAMELS, GOLD, JEWELS, THIS TENT... BUT THEY COULDN'T FIND REAL BELLY DANCERS?
OR REAL MUSICIANS?
I'M GONNA CHECK ON THE CAMELS...
NO MISTRESS, YOU CANNOT GO OUT THERE! NOT UNTIL WE DEAL WITH SOME INTERLOPERS!
IT'S TOO DANGEROUS!
HUH? WHAT? I CAN'T HEAR YOU!
HEY... WHAT ARE THEY DOING?
THAT'S MY MOM!
THEY'RE HURTING MY MOM!
1001 MORE PARDONS, BUT I CANNOT HEAR YOU OVER THE MUSIC, SULTANA!
SAVE MY MOM! MY MOM! MY MOM!
WHY THANK YOU, MISTRESS. SALAAM TO YOU, TOO.

Arwaah...?
GENIE!
PAF

THERE YOU ARE! GENIE! COME HERE!
"Arwaah: a classification of genie known for causing mischief and grief, especially to children..."

HEY, WHADDYA DOIN' THERE? THAT HURTS!
WHAT?! YOU SPEAK ENGLISH? WHY DIDN'T YOU SAY SO?
YOINK!
YOU NEVER ASKED.

WHY YOU--
BY THE EYE OF THE TIGER!
D-DID I NOT GIVE YOU WHAT YOU WISHED FOR?
LISTEN TO ME: MY MOM AND MY FRIENDS ARE IN DANGER!

I HAVE ONE MORE WISH LEFT--
I'LL STOP THE EXECUTION RIGHT AWAY.
NO! THIS ISN'T FUN ANYMO--
OH, YOU WANT TO PLAY THAT CARD!
I WANT--
"EVERYTHING BACK THE WAY IT WAS BEFORE I RUBBED THE LAMP."
UH-HUH. BEEN DOING THIS FOR THOUSANDS OF YEARS. I KNOW THE DRILL...
SIM SIM SALA

BIM!

FIRST THINGS FIRST, LET'S SEE IF THIS THING FLIES!
The End?

Alison Dare & the Secret of the Blue Scarab

OAN'S
DEMY
IRLS
"WE INTERRUPT OUR REGULARLY SCHEDULED PROGRAM FOR A SPECIAL NEWS BULLETIN...
"THE BLUE SCARAB IS DEAD."
"I REPEAT: THE BLUE SCARAB IS DEAD."

I...I DON'T B-BELIEVE IT... IT CAN'T BE...
OH, POOR ALISON...
WE NOW GO TO AN ON-THE-SPOT REPORT AT THE SCENE OF THE TRAGIC EVENT WHICH OCCURRED MOMENTS AGO...

ALISON... DID YOU HEAR THE NEWS?
IT'S JUST PLAIN AWFUL, ALISON.
I NEED A SNACK.
WHAT'S WRONG WITH HER, WENDY? DOESN'T SHE CARE?
I DON'T KNOW, DOT. BUT I WONDER HOW QUICKLY POST-TRAUMATIC STRESS SYNDROME CAN TAKE EFFECT...

DARING ADVENTURES FEATURING The BLUE SCARAB!!

DARING READERS, DO YOU BELIEVE THE WORLD SHALL END IN FIRE? OR ARE YOU OF THE MIND THAT IT WILL END IN ICE? THE ANSWER IS OBVIOUSLY ARCTIC FOR THE SUB-ZERO ANTI-HERO ... AUNTIE FREEZE!
BUTTON UP YOUR OVERCOATS, THERE'S A CHILL IN THE AIR AS THE BLUE SCARAB DISCOVERS...
THE ICE WOMAN COMETH!
I WANT ONE MILLION IN COLD HARD CASH OR THIS ICED BURG WILL REMAIN IN A DEEP FREEZE FOREVER!

C-C-C-CRIME D-DOESN'T P-PAY, Y-YOU I-I-ICE A-AGED O-O-OCTOGENERIAN...
OH, IT PAYS ALL RIGHT!

YOU'LL PAY. YOU'LL ALL PAY--
EXCUSE ME, MA'AM...

MAY I PAY WITH A DEBIT CARD?
THE BLUE SCARAB!
MANNERLY AND MAJESTIC, OUR HERO ARRIVES TO DEFROST AND DETHRONE THE SNOW QUEEN!

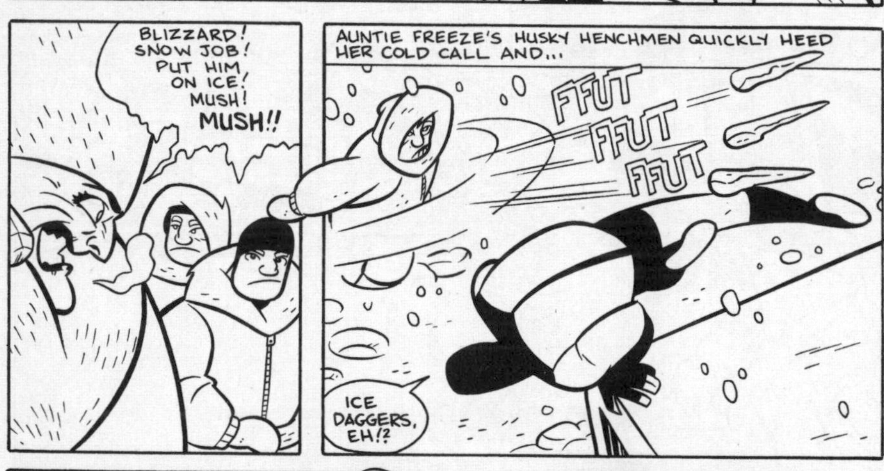
BLIZZARD! SNOW JOB! PUT HIM ON ICE! MUSH! MUSH!!
AUNTIE FREEZE'S HUSKY HENCHMEN QUICKLY HEED HER COLD CALL AND...
FFUT
FFUT
FFUT
ICE DAGGERS, EH!?

BOP!
COME NOW, YOU WINTRY WIMPS ARE GONNA HAVE TO DO BETTER THAN THAT!

SNOWBALLS? SNOWBALLS!?! YOU'VE GOT TO BE KIDDING!
PAF!
PAF!

USING HIS WEATHERPROOF WINGS, SCARAB SENDS A SMALL BUT STINGING SNOWSTORM BACK AT THE BAD GUY.
HOW'D YOU LIKE A FACE FULL OF SNOW, CHILLY WILLY?
WHUMP!

OKAY, SCARAB... FREEZE!

GIVE IT UP, COLDFINGER. YOU CAN'T HURT WHAT YOU CAN'T HIT. I'M TOO FAST FOR YOU.
WHY, SCARAB, WHO SAID ANYTHING ABOUT AIMING MY POLAR PISTOL DIRECTLY AT YOU?
I DON'T WANT TO SHOOT YOU...
7PM 9PM
SNOW WHITE
MIDWINTER'S TALE

I WANT TO BURY YOU!
SKROW
GASP!
THE FROSTY FEMME FATALE UNLEASHES AN AVALANCHE UPON OUR HERO...

MWA-HA HA-HA!
WHO SAYS THE WORLD WILL END IN FIRE? ...IT SURE LOOKS LIKE A BITTER COLD CONCLUSION FOR THE BLUE SCARAB! HAS THE FRIGID FIEND FINALLY FINISHED OFF HER FEARLESS FOE? FIND OUT IN THE NEXT EXCITING ISSUE OF DARING ADVENTURES...

...SHE HAD TO HAVE KNOWN THIS MIGHT HAPPEN SOMEDAY... CONSIDERING HIS LINE OF WORK...
...SURE, BUT ALISON'S REACTING TOO CALMLY... SOMETHING'S WRONG.

Alison's Scrapbook

TALK TO HER, WENDY... YOU'RE BETTER WITH WORDS.
BUT WHAT DO YOU SAY AT A TIME LIKE THIS, DOT?

GIRLS... YOU ALREADY KNOW THE TRUE IDENTITY OF THE BLUE SCARAB...

BUT THERE'S ANOTHER SECRET I SHOULD SHARE WITH YOU...

HAVE I EVER TOLD YOU HOW MY MOM AND DAD MET?

ALICE AND ALAN - EGYPT - 19

Daring Romance
TWO FOREIGNERS IN A FOREIGN LAND, BOTH IN SEARCH OF SOMETHING...
COULD IT BE EXCITEMENT? ADVENTURE? OR MORE, SUCH AS MEANING IN THEIR LIVES?
PERHAPS WHAT THEY'RE LOOKING FOR IS... LOVE.
OPPOSITES ATTRACT BUT SHOULD THESE TWO DARING TRAVELLERS PASS EACH OTHER LIKE SHIPS IN THE NIGHT AND AVOID TROUBLED WATERS AHEAD?
OR DOES THE INTRIGUE PROVE TOO HARD TO RESIST FOR...
LOVERS IN A DANGEROUS TIME

THAT BEAUTIFUL WOMAN... SHE SMILED AT ME... WOW, SHE'S GOT THE BIGGEST, MOST BEAUTIFUL ...EYES I'VE EVER SEEN... I BET SHE'S THE SPUNKY TYPE, TOO...
HMM, HANDSOME... BUT KIND OF SHY... AND THERE'S SOMETHING SWEET AND GENTLE ABOUT HIM... I BET HE'S THE STRONG, SILENT TYPE...

ONE FINDS LOVE WHEN THEY'RE IN THE RIGHT PLACE AT THE RIGHT TIME

FOR THIS YOUNG ARCHAEOLOGY STUDENT WITH AN ADVENTUROUS STREAK, THE RIGHT PLACE IS THIS EGYPTIAN BAZAAR.

FOR THIS THOUGHTFUL LIBRARIAN ON VACATION, THE RIGHT PLACE IS THIS OPEN AIR MARKET AS WELL.

AND THE RIGHT TIME FOR BOTH OF THEM IS NOW...

...OR IS IT?

HOW COULD SOMETHING THAT FEELS SO RIGHT BE SO WRONG?
I HEAR THAT'S A PRETTY GOOD GUIDE BOOK.
THAT'S A NICE BLANKET.

ASK THESE SHADY EMISSARIES...

I TAKE IT. YOU'RE NOT FROM AROUND HERE.
WHAT GAVE ME AWAY?
ARE YOU HERE ON BUSINESS OR PLEASURE?
PLEASURE.

SO WHAT'S YOUR BUSINESS?
I...I'M A... HISTORIAN OF SORTS... UH, DOING SOME PERSONAL RESEARCH FOR A NEW BOOK... --YOU?
I...I'M... KIND OF AN EXPLORER GATHERING SUPPLIES FOR AN EXPEDITION...

AN ADVENTURER... HOW EXCITING...I'M SURE YOU'VE BEEN TO SOME DANGEROUS BUT... BEAUTIFUL PLACES...
A WRITER... HOW FASCINATING ...YOU MUST BE A VERY INTELL-IGENT AND... EXPERIENCED MAN...

SUDDENLY, A BEAUTIFUL MOMENT...
TAP TAP

TURNS UGLY...
MISS DARE, WE HAVE AN IMPORTANT MESSAGE FOR YOU.

WHAT IS THIS?

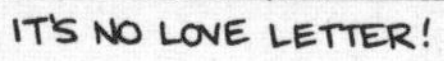

IT'S NO LOVE LETTER!

GASP!
IS EVERYTHING ALL RIGHT?

BUT SOMETIMES EVEN WHEN LOVE IS ILL-FATED IT MUST STILL COME TO PASS...

COME WITH US.
S-SORRY... I HAVE TO GO...

AFTER ALL, 'TIS BETTER TO HAVE LOVED AND LOST THAN NOT TO HAVE LOVED AT ALL...

EVEN IF THAT LOVE IS CATALYZED BY ... DANGER!

TO BE CONTINUED
IN THE NEXT ISSUE OF

OH, IT'S SO ROMANTIC... MEETING IN AN EXOTIC PLACE LIKE THAT...
YEAH, DAD TOLD ME IT WAS LOVE AT FIRST SIGHT FOR HIM.
BUT HE WASN'T SURE HE WAS THE RIGHT MATCH FOR SOMEONE AS EXCITING AND ADVENTUROUS AS MY MOM.
WELL, MAYBE NOT "MR. RIGHT" BUT DEFINITELY "MR. RIGHT NOW." BACK THEN I MEAN.
WAIT A MINUTE... SO YOUR PARENTS LIED TO EACH OTHER ABOUT WHAT THEY DID WHEN THEY FIRST MET?
NOW I SEE WHERE YOU GOT YOUR "GIFT FOR FICTION", ALISON. SUDDENLY IT ALL MAKES SENSE!

YOU KNOW... MOM MIGHT NOT BE AROUND TODAY IF SHE AND DAD HADN'T MET WHEN THEY DID.
I MIGHT NOT BE AROUND!
Grampa

ACTUALLY, NONE OF US WOULD BE HERE!
IF MY FOLKS DIDN'T MEET THE WAY THEY DID, THE BLUE SCARAB MIGHT NEVER HAVE BEEN..."BORN" TO SAVE THE WORLD ALL THOSE TIMES!

HUH? WHAT?

YOU MEAN YOUR MOM HAD SOMETHING TO DO WITH--

I'M GETTING A BIT AHEAD OF MYSELF.
BUT BEFORE I CONTINUE, YOU MUST PROMISE NEVER TO REPEAT TO ANYONE WHAT I'M ABOUT TO TELL YOU. IT'S A MATTER OF NATIONAL SECURITY EVEN!

CROSS YOUR HEART, DARE TO DIE?
DARE TO STICK NEEDLES IN OUR EYES!

HE'S ONLY KNOWN HER
FOR MERE MINUTES
BUT SOMETHING POWERFUL
DRAWS HIM TO HER...

DRAWS HIM INTO
DANGER...
AND INTRIGUE AND...

Daring Romance

AND SO HE FOLLOWS THE MEN WHO TOOK CAPTIVE
THE WOMAN WHO JUST CAPTURED HIS HEART.

NOT REALIZING SOMETHING BIGGER THAN THE
BOTH OF THEM WAS AT WORK HERE.

THAT'S...THE CURSED TOMB OF AKHENATEN! THIS COULD BE MORE SERIOUS THAN I THOUGHT... MAYBE I SHOULD HAVE CALLED THE AUTHORITIES...

I TOLD YOU... I DON'T KNOW HOW TO OPEN IT.
ZAT IS EXACTLY VAT YOUR FAZA SAID, MISS DARE.
VOULD YOU LIKE TO KNOW VUT VE DID TO ZE FAMED DR. ARCHEMEDES DARE AFTER HE TOLD US ZAT?

Ptew

SLAP!
THAT MONSTER!

ANY MAN WOULD BE AGHAST AT SEEING SUCH A VILLAIN RAISE A HAND TO A WOMAN!
I'VE SEEN ENOUGH!
SMASH

BUT A HERO WOULD NOT STAND TO SEE HER HARMED FURTHER...
THAT'S NO WAY TO TREAT A LADY!

AND AS EVERYONE KNOWS HEROES AREN'T BORN BUT MADE...
OOF!
PAF!

LEAVE HIM ALONE, YOU BEAST!

RECALL THAT ADAGE ABOUT BEING IN THE RIGHT PLACE...
CAN'T LET... THESE... EVIL... MEN DO THIS...

AT THE RIGHT TIME!
SHUNK!

UND NOW VE ARE GETTINK SOMEVHERE.
WHOEVER YOU ARE, HERO, I SUGGEST YOU... HOW DO ZEY SAY IN ZE MOVIES... "FREEZE" VHERE YOU ARE.

YOU, ON ZE OZZER HAND, MISS DARE, VILL BE SO KIND AS TO RETRIEVE FOR ME ZE AMULET FROM ZE TOMB.

NO! YOU CAN'T GO IN THERE! THE CURSE...
I HAVE NO CHOICE. I'LL RISK ANY CURSE TO SAVE MY FATHER.

YOU VESTERNERS ARE SUPPOZED TO BE SCIENTIFIC... PROGREZIVE ZINKINK UND MODERN. NOT SUPERSTITIOUS...
THEN YOU GO IN THERE!

I AM NOT FROM ZE VEST. UND I SUGGEST YOU HURRY, MISS DARE. YOUR FAZA DOES NOT HAVE MUCH TIME LEFT.
STOP!
PROMISE NOT TO HARM HER AND I'LL GO...
WHAT AM I LOOKING FOR?
YOU ARE LOOKINK FOR ZIS: ZE AMULET OF ZE BLUE SCARAB.
IT IS SAID TO CONTAIN ZE POWER OF ZE GODS ZEMSELVES.
NO... PLEASE... THE CURSE... LET ME GO IN...
THINK OF YOUR FATHER ... IF ANYTHING SHOULD HAPPEN TO YOU WHO'LL SAVE HIM?
I-I DON'T EVEN KNOW YOUR NAME.
IT'S ALAN. ALAN DODD. AND I LIED ABOUT BEING A "HISTORIAN"... I'M JUST A LIBRARIAN ON HOLIDAY...
MY NAME IS ALICE ... AND I'M JUST AN ARCHAEOLOGY STUDENT TAGGING ALONG WITH HER FAMOUS FATHER ON AN EXCAVATION...

ENOUGH VIS ZE CONFESSIONS!
TAKE ZIS UND GO GET ZE AMULET, "SUPERHERO"...

AND SO, THE LIBRARIAN ENTERS THE UNKNOWN, UNSURE IF HE'LL EVER SEE HIS NEW LOVE'S FACE EVER AGAIN...
...AND YET KNOWING SHOULD HE PERISH SO THAT SHE MAY LIVE, IT WOULD BE WORTH THE FLEETING TIME THEY SHARED!

MOMENTS LATER...

IF I'M NOT MISTAKEN... THIS IS FROM "THE BOOK OF THE DEAD"!
"HAIL, ATEN, LORD OF LIGHT, WHEN THOU SHINEST, ALL RIGHTEOUS SOULS LIVE ON."

I'D LOVE TO STAY AND INVESTIGATE THIS PLACE MORE...
...BUT THIS IS WHAT I CAME FOR!

SUDDENLY...
WHAT THE--?!
RUMBLE

MEANWHILE...
WHAT'S HAPPENING?
IT'S THE CURSE! THE CURSE OF AKHENATEN!
RUMBLE RUMBLE
AAAAH
ALAN...
HAIL, ATEN...
LORD OF LIGHT...
WHEN THOU SHINEST...
ALL RIGHTEOUS SOULS LIVE ON.

ALAN!
NOOOOOOo
"HAIL ATEN
LORD OF LIGHT...
"WHEN THOU SHINEST,
ALL RIGHTEOUS SOULS...
"...LIVE ON"
I'VE GOT YOU!
YOU'VE GOT ME...
BUT WHO'S GOT YOU?!

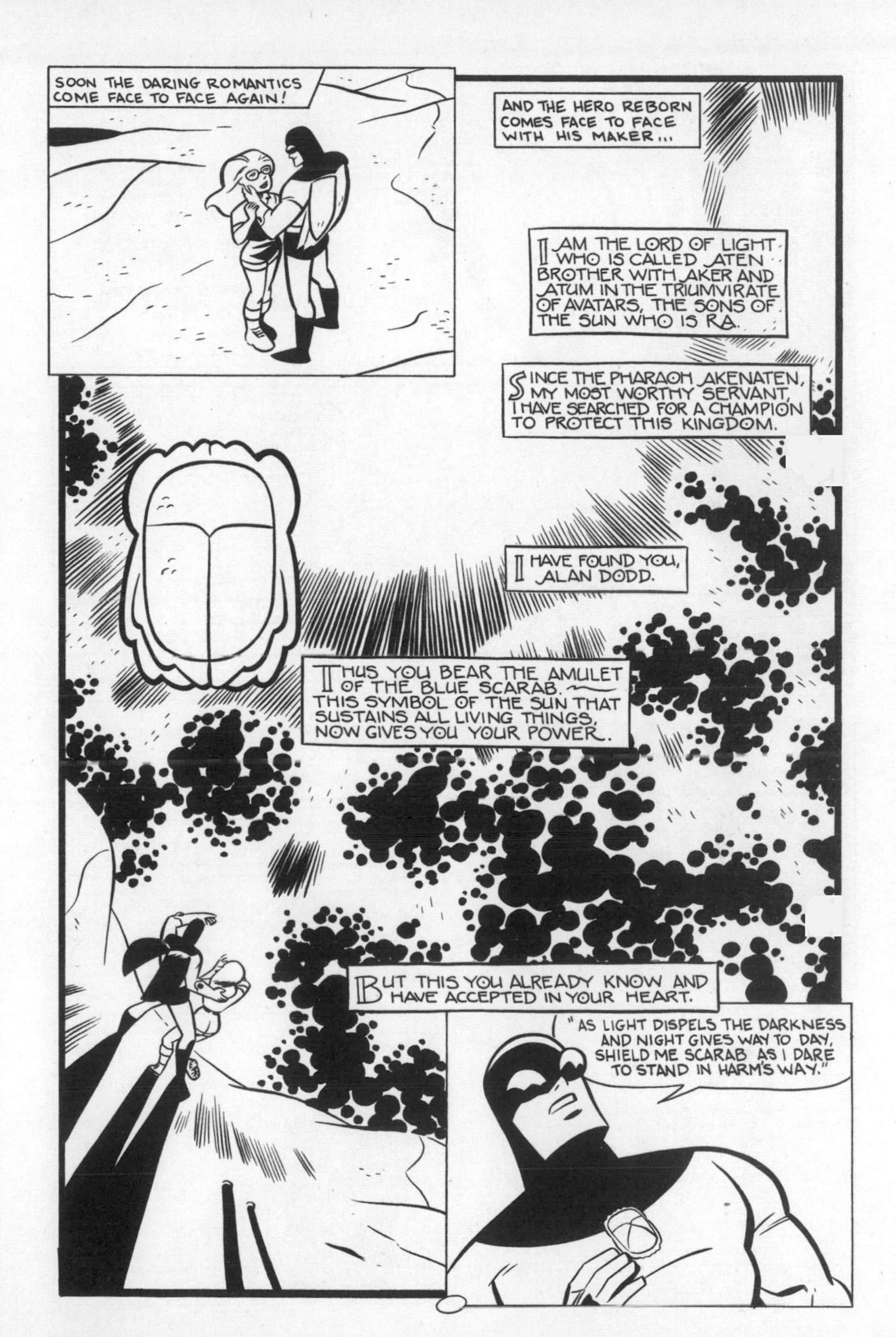
SOON THE DARING ROMANTICS COME FACE TO FACE AGAIN!
AND THE HERO REBORN COMES FACE TO FACE WITH HIS MAKER...
I AM THE LORD OF LIGHT WHO IS CALLED ATEN BROTHER WITH AKER AND ATUM IN THE TRIUMVIRATE OF AVATARS, THE SONS OF THE SUN WHO IS RA.
SINCE THE PHARAOH AKENATEN, MY MOST WORTHY SERVANT, I HAVE SEARCHED FOR A CHAMPION TO PROTECT THIS KINGDOM.
I HAVE FOUND YOU, ALAN DODD.
THUS YOU BEAR THE AMULET OF THE BLUE SCARAB. THIS SYMBOL OF THE SUN THAT SUSTAINS ALL LIVING THINGS, NOW GIVES YOU YOUR POWER.
BUT THIS YOU ALREADY KNOW AND HAVE ACCEPTED IN YOUR HEART.
"AS LIGHT DISPELS THE DARKNESS AND NIGHT GIVES WAY TO DAY, SHIELD ME SCARAB AS I DARE TO STAND IN HARM'S WAY."

SURELY AS THE SUN RISES, ALAN DODD, YOU SHALL ALWAYS TRIUMPH OVER THE EVIL THAT MEN DO.
...AND AS LONG AS YOU WEAR THE AMULET, YOU CAN NOT PERISH BY THE HAND OF VILLAINY
YOU ARE A PROTECTOR OF THE KINGDOM...
YOU ARE A CHAMPION OF THE PEOPLE...
YOU ARE A LIGHT IN THE DARKNESS.

YOU ARE... THE BLUE SCARAB?
LIKE IN THE LEGENDS?
BUT THAT MEANS YOU HAD TO HAVE DIED A VICTIM OF EVIL DEEDS, AND THEN...

I WAS REBORN BY THE POWER OF RA, YES.
YOU LOOK GOOD FOR SOMEONE JUST BACK FROM THE DEAD.

YOU DON'T LOOK SO BAD YOURSELF, "MISS DARE."

SIGH. I WANT TO MEET THAT SPECIAL SOMEONE WHILE ON SOME WILD ADVENTURE, TOO... HMM BUT WHAT WOULD I WEAR?
I REALLY HOPE YOUR MOM AND DAD GET BACK TOGETHER SOON, ALISON.
OH, THEY WILL... IF I HAVE ANYTHING TO DO WITH IT.

I THINK I'M BEGINNING TO UNDERSTAND WHAT YOU'RE TRYING TO TELL US...
I HAVE SOMETHING HERE ABOUT THE SCARAB BEETLE, ALSO KNOWN AS SCARABAEUS SACER, THE DUNG BEETLE.

WENDY! MY DAD IS NO DUNG BEETLE!
WAIT... IT SAYS HERE THAT TO ANCIENT EGYPTIANS THE SCARAB BEETLE WAS A SACRED SYMBOL REPRESENTING THE SUN, LIFE, SELF-GENERATION, AND SELF-RENEWAL.

THEY ALSO BELIEVED THAT A SCARAB PUSHED THE SUN LIKE A DISK ACROSS THE SKY, CAUSING SUNRISES AND SUNSETS.
I DID NOT KNOW THAT!

WELL, THAT'S SOME NIFTY SCIENCE FICTION, BUT WHAT DOES THAT HAVE TO DO WITH YOUR DAD?

DON'T YOU GET IT, DOT? MY DADDY'S INVINCIBLE!
AS LONG AS HE WEARS THE AMULET HE CAN'T "PERISH BY THE HAND OF VILLAINY."
BUT THE NEWS REPORT SAID YOUR FATHER WAS CRUSHED TO DEATH UNDER AN AVALANCHE OF ICE AND SNOW!
MR. DODD HAS THE SELF-GENERATING, SELF-RENEWING POWERS OF THE MAGICAL SCARABAEUS SACER!

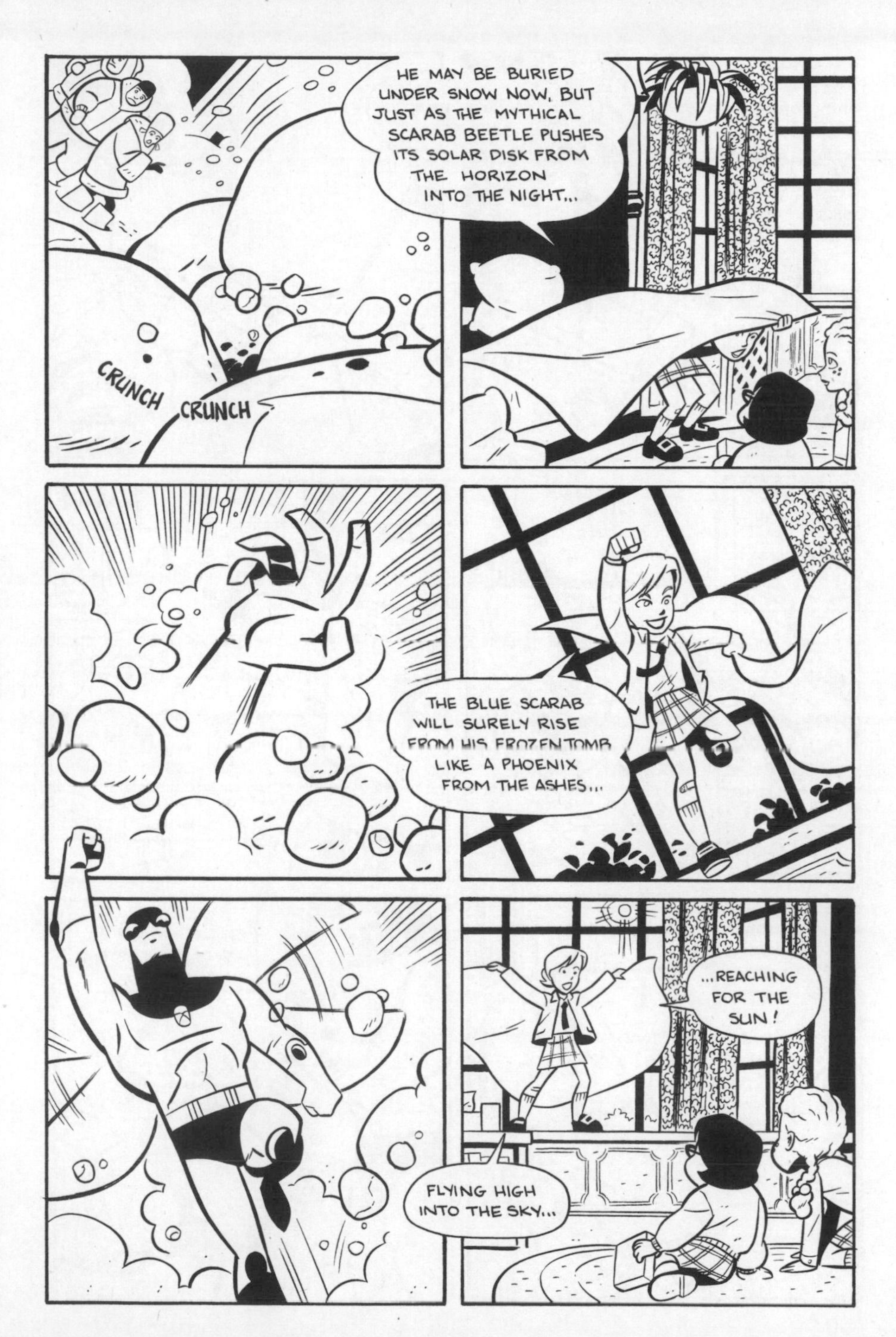
HE MAY BE BURIED UNDER SNOW NOW, BUT JUST AS THE MYTHICAL SCARAB BEETLE PUSHES ITS SOLAR DISK FROM THE HORIZON INTO THE NIGHT...
CRUNCH
CRUNCH
THE BLUE SCARAB WILL SURELY RISE FROM HIS FROZEN TOMB LIKE A PHOENIX FROM THE ASHES...
...REACHING FOR THE SUN!
FLYING HIGH INTO THE SKY...

AND SOON AFTER THAT, HE'S GOING AFTER AUNTIE FREEZE...
SHE WON'T BELIEVE HER OWN EYES...
!
SHE'LL PROBABLY MAKE ONE LAST DESPERATE ATTEMPT...
"BUT IT WILL BE IN VAIN..."
"AS LIGHT DISPELS THE DARKNESS AND NIGHT GIVES WAY TO DAY...
" THE AMULET WILL SHIELD MY DAD AS HE DARES TO STAND IN HARM'S WAY."

POW!
AND THAT, MY FRIENDS, IS THE SECRET OF THE BLUE SCARAB!

YOU ARE A PROTECOR OF THE KINGDOM.
YOU ARE A CHAMPION OF THE PEOPLE.
YOU ARE A LIGHT IN THE DARKNESS.

YOUR DAD WOULDN'T HIT A WOMAN, THOUGH, WOULD HE?
NAH, PROBABLY NOT. EVEN IF SHE IS A SUPER-VILLAIN. HE'D FIND THE "GENTLEMANLY" WAY TO STOP HER.

HE WOULDN'T HIT A LADY, BUT WOULD HE BREAK HER HAIR DRYER?

GIRLS! DID YOU HEAR? THE BLUE SCARAB IS ALIVE!
HE'S ALL RIGHT AND HE'S TAKEN AUNTIE FREEZE INTO CUSTODY.

THE MEDIA WAS A BIT PREMATURE IN REPORTING HIS DEATH.

LATER THAT NIGHT...

ALISON? WHAT ARE YOU DOING? TELL ME YOU'RE NOT SNEAKING OUT TONIGHT...

NO, I'M NOT GOING OUT...

I'M LETTING SOMETHING IN!

GASP!
LOCUSTS! THE LOCUSTS ARE BACK!

RELAX. IT'S NOT A LOCUST.

IT'S JUST A MESSAGE FROM MY DAD.

"The reports of my death are greatly exaggerated"
So what movie do you want to see this Saturday?
Love Dad

HEE-HEE. HE QUOTED MARK TWAIN...
WHO?
YOU KNOW, "TOM SAWYER" AND "HUCKLEBERRY FINN."
OH... I DON'T LIKE PIE...

THERE, A QUICK REPLY AND IT'S BACK TO BED FOR EVERYONE.
WHAT DID YOU WRITE?

OH, COME ON, LET A GIRL KEEP ONE SECRET...
THE END

Alison Dare & the Mummy Child

AMY!
START THE
PLANE!

START THE PLANE, AMY!

SO ONCE AGAIN, DR.DARE, VAT VAS BRIEFLY YOURS IS NOW MINE.

WHOOP
WHOOP
WHOOP

SCHNELL! GIVE ME ZE CHILD UND I'LL LET YOU LIVE.

YOU'D BE OUT OF BUSINESS IF YOU KILLED ME, BARON!

IT'S ALWAYS A SHAME VEN A WOMAN MUST CHOOSE BETWEEN A BABY UND HER CAREER-
MWA-HA-HA-HA!
OH!
ALICE! ARE YOU ALL RIGHT?
MY baby...

YOUR MOTHER WAS RUNNING AROUND THE ANDES WHILE SHE WAS PREGNANT WITH YOU?
THAT MIGHT ACTUALLY EXPLAIN A FEW THINGS...
MOM SAYS THE FIRST TIME SHE FELT ME KICK WAS WHILE SHE WATCHED BARON VON BARON GET AWAY WITH THE FIRST MUMMY CHILD SHE FOUND.
I GUESS I WAS JUST AS ANGRY WITH THAT NASTY NAZI AS MY MOM WAS!
COOL.
YOU KNOW, I'D LIKE TO WRITE A COMPARITIVE PAPER ON THE MUMMIFICATION TECHNIQUES OF THE INCAS VERSUS THAT OF THE ANCIENT EGYPTIANS...
IT'S SO MORBID BUT I'M THOROUGHLY FASCINATED BY THE RITUALISTIC SACRIFICIAL RITES OF THE INCAS.
I DON'T KNOW WHAT "MORBID" MEANS, I JUST WANNA SEE THE DEAD KID!

MUSEUM
OPENING SOON
TREASURES OF THE INCA
SEE THE MUMMY CHILD
UM... DID YOU PAY THE DRIVER, ALISON?

JENNY
NICKEL TRAIN MUSEUM
ALISON! THE CAB'S DRIVING AWAY BUT NO ONE PAID THE FARE...

ALISON! WE DIDN'T PAY FOR THE TAXI! SHOULDN'T WE DO THE HONEST THING AND CALL THE DISPATCH-
THAT WASN'T JUST ANY CAB DRIVER- THAT WAS MY UNCLE JOHNNY!

I THOUGHT HE WAS SUPPOSED TO LOOK DASHING AND RUGGED AND DEVILISHLY HANDSOME...
THAT CREEPY MUSTACHE HAS GOT TO GO!

IT'S CALLED A DISGUISE! HOW ELSE CAN HE "VISIT" ME AND NOT REVEAL HIS SECRET IDENTITY TO ANY ONE OF A HUNDRED CRIMINAL ADVERSARIES BENT ON EXACTING THEIR REVENGE ON HIM?

VAT ARE YOU KIDS DOINGK HERE? ZE MUSEUM IS CLOSINGK. YOU MUST GET OUT, JA?

MY MOM IS EXPECTING ME!

OUT, OUT, OUT... SCHNELL!

WHAT'S WITH YOU TODAY? AND THAT KOOKY ACCENT!

WHERE HAVE YOU TWO BEEN STOP ZAT BRAT!
YIKES! WHO ARE THOSE BRUTES?

UH-OH,...
...THIS DOESN'T LOOK GOOD.

I TOLD YOU, I WASN'T EXPECTING ALISON TODAY.
BUT SHE CALLED AND ASKED ME TO PICK HER UP HERE!

LOOK, I HAVE NO IDEA WHAT'S GOING ON. SHE WAS SUPPOSED TO SPEND THIS WEEKEND WITH YOU.
SHE TOLD ME YOU WANTED TO SPEND SOME TIME WITH HER.

TODAY, ALAN? WITH ONLY DAYS LEFT BEFORE THE OPENING? MAYBE YOU HAVEN'T NOTICED FROM THIS MESS BUT WE'RE BEHIND SCHEDULE. THAT MUDSLIDE OUTSIDE LIMA DELAYED SOME SHIPMENTS.

OKAY, GO AHEAD AND BLAME ME FOR THAT, TOO, ALICE...

sigh I'M NOT BLAMING ANYTHING ON YOU.
I'M JUST REALLY BUSY WITH THIS NEW EXHIBIT. YOU KNOW HOW IMPORTANT THIS IS. IT'S BEEN A LONG TIME COMING...
COULD YOU JUST... SPEAK TO YOUR DAUGHTER, HUH?
SHE'S YOUR DAUGHTER, TOO.

WHAT'S THAT SUPPOSED TO MEAN?
MOM! DAD! HIYA, GUYS!
ALISON! YOU TOLD ME YOU WERE SPENDING THE AFTERNOON HERE.
BUT YOU DIDN'T TELL *ME* ABOUT IT.
SO WHERE HAVE YOU BEEN?!
YOU'VE BEEN...
...ON A PICNIC?
OKAY... I CONFESS, I PLANNED ALL OF THIS...

VELL, VELL ... VOULDN'T ZIS MAKE A LOVELY FAMILY PHOTO.
IS THIS ALSO PART OF YOUR PLAN?
THE GIRLS CAME WITH ME. DON'T KNOW WHO THE HEAVIES ARE. OR WHAT'S UP WITH FRECKLES AND THE ACCENT...
WHO ARE THESE MEN? WENDY? DOT?
... DR. DARE...
...help...
WHAT'S GOING ON HERE...?
RIIIPP!

IT'S A GENERAL COURTESY TO INVITE YOUR COLLEAGUES TO SEE YOUR NEW EXHIBITS, DR. DARE.
BARON VON BARON!

I VAS SO HURT WHEN YOU DIDN'T CALL.
FIRST OF ALL, WE'RE NOT COLLEAGUES...

COLLEAGUES, COMPETITION - ZAME DIFFERENCE, MY DEAR.

SECONDLY, THE SHOW'S NOT OPENING TILL THE END OF THE WEEK!
OH, GOOD. I AM NOT MISSING IT YET, JA? TOO BAD ZE STAR ATTRACTION VILL BE...
NO! YOU'RE NOT GONNA TAKE ANOTHER ONE AWAY FROM ME!
OH YES, I VILL, DR. DARE.
I'VE BEEN FOLLOWING YOU CLOSELY EVER SINCE I READ ABOUT YOUR RETURN TO THE ANDES FOUR MONTHS AGO. I KNEW YOU'D EVENTUALLY LOCATE ZE UZZER MUMMY CHILD.

ITS TWIN, ZE ONE I TOOK FROM YOU VAT VAS IT? TEN YEARS AGO? SHE MISSES HER SISTER.
IT'S ABOUT TIME ZEY WERE REUNITED, JA?
YOU COULDN'T GET THE HAND OF HAEPHESTUS TO WORK. AND THE BLACK BUUK DIDN'T RAISE THAT ARMY OF DEAD YOU WANTED...
BUT YOU'VE DISCOVERED ANOTHER WAY OF GAINING SUPER-NATURAL POWERS USING THESE MUMMIES, HAVEN'T YOU?
MAYBE ZAT'S WHY.
WHO IS KNOWINK FOR SURE?
I AM HOW YOU ZAY, A RIDDLE WRAPPED IN AN ENIGMA CONTAINED IN A CONUNDRUM.
OR MAYBE I JUST HAVE A THINK FOR TWINS.

WE'VE GOT YOUR TWINS RIGHT HERE, BARON.
I'M SURE YOU DO.
BUT LOOK WHAT I'VE GOT!
ALISON!
NOW... STEP ASIDE, MY YOUNG HERO MAN. AND TELL YOUR ... BIG SISTER TO BE DROPPINK ZE CROWBAR UND LET MY MEN DO ZER VORK.

SMASH

AGAIN VE ZEE ZERE IS NOTHING YOU CAN POSSESS WHICH I CANNOT TAKE AWAY, DR. DARE.

ALISON... DON'T DO ANYTHING... FOOLISH. YOU HEAR ME?

AIM THAT ARMAMENT ELSEWHERE, ADOLPH!
MAYBE I SHOULD HAVE SAID SOMETHING TO JOCK...

CHOMP!
AIEEE!
ALISON! YOU AND THE GIRLS, GET OUT OF HERE...
BUT-
NOW!

BANG!
AS ZEY SAY IN ZE MOVIES, EVERYBODY... FREEZE!

I ZAID, FREEZE!
I'LL GET'EM, BOSS!

WHY DOESN'T YOUR DAD JUST TURN INTO THE BLUE SCARAB?
MEDIEVAL EXHIBIT
THAT WOULD -gasp- REVEAL HIS... SECRET IDENTITY TO ALL THOSE PEOPLE -huff puff-

LISTEN, YOU GUYS CALL THE POLICE. I'M GOING BACK TO TRY AND CAUSE A DISTRACTION OR SOMETHING. GIVE MY DAD A CHANCE TO CHANGE.
THAT'S TOO DANGEROUS, ALISON!

AND WHAT'S MY MIDDLE NAME, WENDY?
ISN'T IT... ATHENA?
OH, NEVER MIND!

GASP! SOMEONE'S COMING!
NO TIME TO ARGUE! GET HELP!

LOOKING FOR SOMEONE?
CREAK

NEXT TIME, ALICE DARE, IT WILL TAKE MORE THAN... CHILDREN TO SAVE YOU.

WHO YOU CALLING A CHILD, YOU OLD RELIC!
EASY, JOCK...

...THE AMULET...
NO... NOT OUT IN THE OPEN LIKE THIS...

I LOST THE OTHER TWO, BOSS.
NEVER MIND ZEM. GIVE ME ZE BAG. UND HURRY, VE HAVE VASTED ENOUGH TIME...

BAG?

JA! ZE BAG FOR TRANSPORTING ZE MUMMY, DUMMY.
UH... I MUST HAVE DROPPED IT CHASING AFTER THIS ONE...
HEY, I HAVE A PICNIC BLANKET YOU COULD USE!

ALISON... WHAT ARE YOU UP TO...?

OH BARON...

I SEE WHERE YOU'RE GOING WITH THIS, ALI-OOP.
GO FOR IT, KID!

SPLAT
DID SHE JUST DO WHAT I THINK SHE DID?
YEP. CLASSIC "PIE-IN-THE-FACE" ROUTINE.
W-WHAT ARE YOU DOING, VINNIE? LET GO OF THE BOSS...
HEY!
...COOL IT WITH THAT GUN, MISTER!
CRASH!
PSHHHT
ALISON ACTUALLY HAD A SELTZER BOTTLE IN THE PICNIC BASKET!
GOOD TO SEE YOU AGAIN, ALAN
LIKEWISE, JOHNNY.
ZIS IS A COCONUT CREAM PIE! I AM ALLERGIC TO ZE COCO-NUT!
ACK!

MY BABY...
OH-NO...

MY POOR BABY...
ALL THAT GLASS...
AND THE FALL...

HERE, MOM. USE THIS TO CLEAN HER UP...

DOESN'T LOOK LIKE THERE'S ANY REAL DAMAGE THOUGH.

WHEW. THAT'S GOOD.

COME HERE...

DOES SHE HAVE A NAME?
WOULD YOU LIKE TO NAME HER?

HOW ABOUT... ATHENA!

DO YOU THINK YOU CAN GET YOUR OTHER "BABY" BACK FROM THE BARON NOW?
I HOPE SO. BUT IF NOT, I HAVE THE ONLY BABY I'LL EVER NEED RIGHT HERE.
AND I'M NOT TALKING ABOUT "ATHENA"...

HIYA, SIS.
LONG TIME NO SEE, LITTLE BROTHER.

SOME FAMILY REUNION THIS TURNED OUT TO BE, HUH?
ISN'T UNCLE JOHNNY'S DISGUISE AMAZING? HE WAS A CAB DRIVER BEFORE, AND YOU MISSED HIM AS A "KNIGHT IN SHINING ARMOUR."

SIGH. NO, I WOULDN'T SAY I MISSED A THING.
GEEZ, GILLIAN...!

AROOOOOOO
SIRENS.
THAT'S MY CUE.

CAN'T YOU STAY JUST A BIT LONGER, UNCLE JOHNNY? THE PIE'S RUINED BUT I'VE STILL GOT SANDWICHES AND CHIPS AND SOME WATERMELON...
SORRY, MY L'IL MONKEY. GOTTA JET. BUT I'LL BE AT YOUR SCHOOL PLAY NEXT MONTH. LOOK IN THE AUDIENCE FOR THE MAN IN THE YELLOW HAT.

PAF

IT WAS NICE SEEING YOU GUYS AND DOLLS AGAIN. I'LL BE BACK, BUT FOR NOW IT'S TIME FOR ME TO...

WHIRRR
GO, JOHNNY, GO!

SO...
ANYONE ELSE UP FOR A PICNIC?
I'D LOVE TO, ALISON... BUT LOOK AT THIS PLACE... WE WERE BEHIND SCHEDULE AS IT WAS... I'M SORRY...

DR. DARE, YOU CAN TAKE A "BREAK." WE'LL HOLD DOWN THE FORT.
BUT THE POLICE WILL WANT STATEMENTS...

I THINK WE CAN HANDLE IT, DOC.
WELL...

THE END

Also available by J. Torres and J. Bone:

ALISON DARE

THE HEART OF THE MAIDEN

Alison Dare, the daughter of masked superhero the Blue Scarab and famous archaeologist Dr. Alice Dare, is back with her BFF's, Wendy and Dot!

It's lights out at St. Joan's Academy for Girls, and Alison, Wendy, and Dot have already snuck out of their dorms on a mission to find adventure and fun. When the girls discover a hidden chamber tucked beneath the statue of Joan of Arc that stands on the boarding school's lawn, they decide to head down the tunnel to find out what lies below. Once there, the girls find Mother Superior and the other nuns gathered together. Careful not to make a sound, Alison, Wendy, and Dot listen in: Who is the new sister at St. Joan's Academy? And what is the "Heart of the Maiden"? It's clear that Mother Superior and the new sister share a secret. Alison Dare and her friends boldly set off to reveal it, and in the process, they uncover an ancient mystery deep behind the walls of the Academy.

Alison Dare was nominated for the prestigious Eisner Award in the Best Title for a Younger Audience category.

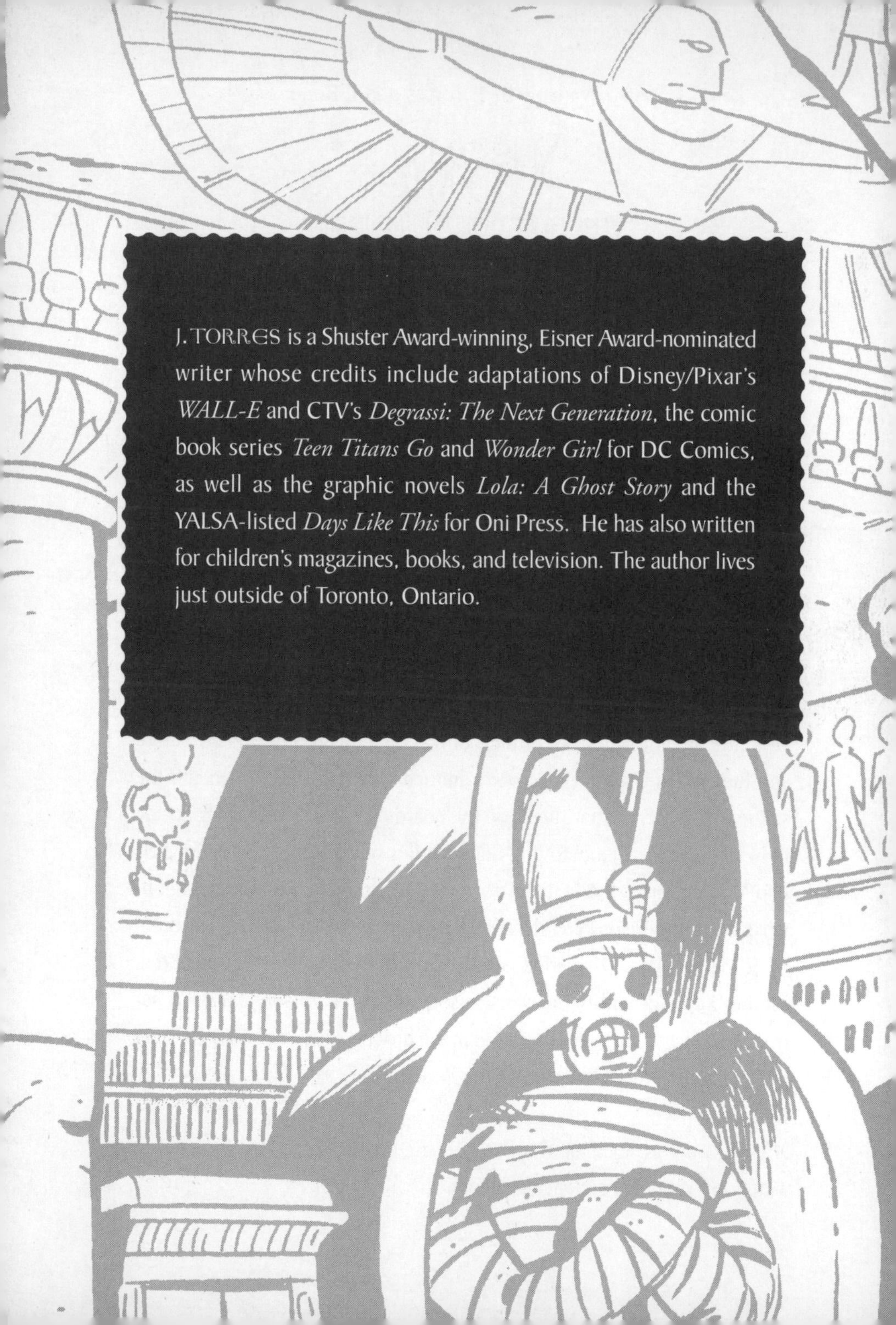

J. TORRES is a Shuster Award-winning, Eisner Award-nominated writer whose credits include adaptations of Disney/Pixar's *WALL-E* and CTV's *Degrassi: The Next Generation*, the comic book series *Teen Titans Go* and *Wonder Girl* for DC Comics, as well as the graphic novels *Lola: A Ghost Story* and the YALSA-listed *Days Like This* for Oni Press. He has also written for children's magazines, books, and television. The author lives just outside of Toronto, Ontario.

J.BONE is an Eisner Award-nominated illustrator of several critically acclaimed comic books and graphic novels, including *Spiderman: Tangled Web*, *Batman / The Spirit*, and Paul Dini's *Mutant, Texas*. J. Bone lives in Toronto, Ontario.